Fox and Owl's Winter Adventure

Jackie Lui

Moonlie

words&pictures

© 2025 Quarto Publishing Group USA Inc.
Text by Jackie Lui
Illustrations © 2025 Moonlie Fong Whittaker

First published in 2025 by words & pictures,
an imprint of The Quarto Group.
100 Cummings Center, Suite 265D
Beverly, MA 01915, USA.
T (978) 282-9590 F (978) 283-2742
www.quarto.com

EEA Representation, W TS Tax d.o.o., Ž anova ulica 3, 4 000 K ranj, Slovenia

Editor: Jackie Lui
Senior Editor: Molly Mead
Designers: Mike Henson and Katharine Radcliffe
Creative Director: Malena Stojić
Associate Publisher: Holly Willsher
Senior Production Controller: Nikki Ingram

No part of this publication may be reproduced, stored
in a retrieval system, or transmitted in any form, or by any
means, electrical, mechanical, photocopying, recording or
otherwise, without the prior written permission of the
publisher or a license permitting restricted copying.
All rights reserved.

ISBN: 978-1-83600-958-0

9 8 7 6 5 4 3 2 1

Manufactured in Guangdong, China TT072025

Fox and Owl's Winter Adventure

Jackie Lui

Moonlie

words&pictures

On a frosty winter night, Ember the fox woke up in the cozy warmth of her underground den.

She was eager to start her day, but her family was still curled up, fast asleep.

"I'll play outside until they wake up," she thought.

She quietly climbed over the snoring foxes and tiptoed out into the woods. The fresh, cold air made her feel wide awake.

"Wow!" she whispered, as her eyes took in the sparkling snow. The whole world looked like it had been sprinkled with glitter.

Next, she trotted toward the big oak tree nearby, her paws crunching on the snow-covered ground.

Ember couldn't wait to play. She laughed with delight as she jumped about and rolled around.

"Hello, Flint!" Ember called. "Look at the snow! It's like everything's sleeping under a big blanket!"

"It is! The wood is so peaceful tonight," Flint replied.

"Look, Ember! Some tracks in the snow—shall we follow them?"

"Yes, let's see where they lead!" she said, nodding excitedly.

She skipped along the path as Flint flew high above, disappearing among the trees and reappearing in the moonlit sky.

"Wait for me!" Ember called.

Flint swooped down. "Oops, I forgot foxes don't have wings," he giggled.

They reached a wide clearing in the woods, where a thick sheet of snow sat undisturbed.

"I've never seen snow so perfect!" said Ember.

"Let's make something beautiful with it!" Flint replied.

The two friends thought for a moment about what to make . . .

"I have an idea," said Ember, her tail wagging.
"Let's make sculptures!"

"I'll make a snow fox!" Flint hooted with excitement.
"And I'll build a snow owl!" Ember said happily.

After choosing the perfect spot,
they began rolling and shaping the snow.

Ember tilted her head. "My snow owl needs big, wise eyes, like yours!" She dashed off to the trees to find some pine cones.

Flint fluffed his wings. "And my snow fox needs something bright and cheerful like your red fur!"

He flew off to find just the right touch of color.

"They're perfect!" Flint said.

"They're wonderful!" Ember agreed.

As the two friends admired their sculptures, the sky began to lighten. An orange glow was creeping up from the horizon.

Suddenly, Ember's ears drooped. "Is everything ok?" Flint asked his friend.

"Once the sun comes up, our beautiful sculptures will melt, and we'll never see them again . . ."

Flint smiled softly. "That's true, but we'll always have this memory. I'll never forget how much fun we had today."

Ember thought for a moment, then her tail wagged. "I'll never forget it either. Thanks, Flint, I'm so happy you're my friend!"

As the sun rose, the pair made their way home.

Ember couldn't wait to tell her family about the sculptures!

What a perfect winter adventure.

Did You Know?

Red fox

Facts about Foxes

Learn more about Ember and Flint and their furry and feathered friends!

- There are lots of different types of foxes. Ember is a red fox. She has a bushy tail, orangey-red fur and white patches on her ears, tail, and tummy.

- Other types of foxes include Arctic foxes, which have white fur and live near the North Pole, and fennec foxes, which are very small and live in the desert.

- It's rare to see a red fox in the daytime because they're usually sleeping. They prefer to have adventures at dawn, when it gets light, and dusk, when it gets dark.

- Foxes like to live in dens where it's cozy and warm. Usually underground, their dens are a safe place for them to rest and take care of their babies, called cubs.

- Just like Ember, fox cubs love having fun. Foxes that live in towns and cities have even been spotted playing on children's trampolines!

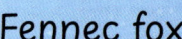
Fennec fox

Arctic fox

Fox den

Tawny owl

Pygmy owl

Facts about Owls

- There are many different types of owls. Flint is a tawny owl. He has big round eyes, fluffy brown-and-white feathers, and makes a 'hoo-hoo-hoo-hoo' sound.

- Other types of owls include barn owls, which have a heart-shaped face and live near farms, and northern pygmy owls, which have yellow eyes and nest in forests.

- Tawny owls are nocturnal, which means they mainly come out at night. Luckily, their big eyes mean that they can see in the dark.

- Owls are a type of bird, so their babies hatch from eggs. Baby tawny owls are called owlets and are often born in a tree hollow.

- Just like human babies, owlets need lots of sleep. They usually snooze on their bellies and snuggle up to their brothers and sisters to keep warm.

Owlets

Barn owl

Awesome Owls

Follow Flint's instructions to make your very own paper owl.
If you're finding some steps tricky, ask your grown-up for help.

You will need:

Three toilet-paper tubes

One long cardboard tube

Paint, including brown and green

Felt, including orange

Six googly eyes

Thick cardstock

Scissors

Glue

Paintbrush

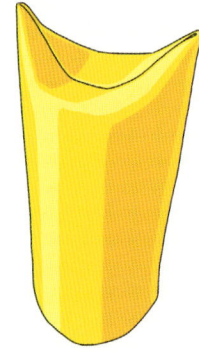

1. To make each owl, push in the sides of the top of a toilet-paper tube, and paint it your favorite color.

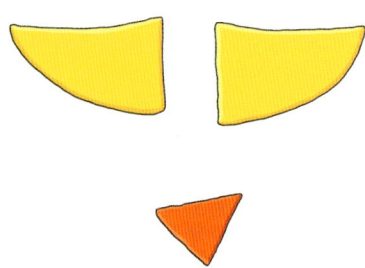

2. From the felt, cut out two wings and an orange beak.

3. Cut out a circle of felt and glue it to the front of the tube. Glue the wings on either side.

4. Glue the beak above the felt circle. Cut out two more circles of felt—they should be slightly larger than the googly eyes. Glue the eyes to the circles of felt, then glue these to your owl.

Repeat steps 1 to 4 to make two more owls.

5. Cut out some branches from the thick cardstock.

6. To make your tree, glue the branches to the back of a long cardboard tube. Paint the tree brown.

7. Cut a circle from the thick cardstock and paint it green. Glue the tree to the green circle. Perch your owls on the tree branches and wait for the hooting to start.

To help your owls sit in their tree, cut two small slits at the bottom of each tube and slot them on to the branches.

Hoo-hoo-hoo-hoo!

Hoo-hoo-hoo-hoo!

Sparkling Snowflake

If you love the snow as much as Ember, follow her instructions to craft a beautiful snowflake.

You will need:

Eight narrow sticks with side shoots

Thick cardstock

White paint

Dried spices, such as cloves, cardamom, and star anise

Stick-on sparkly gems

Scissors

Glue

Paintbrush

1. Cut the eight sticks roughly the same length. Paint them white.

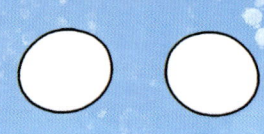

2. Cut out two circles from the thick cardstock. Paint them white.

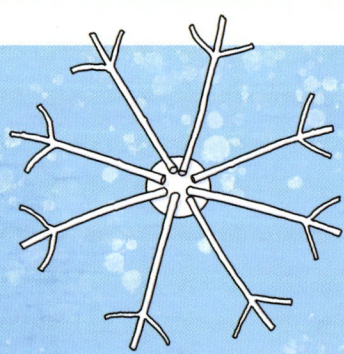

3. Once dry, glue the straight ends of the sticks on to one of the circles of cardstock.

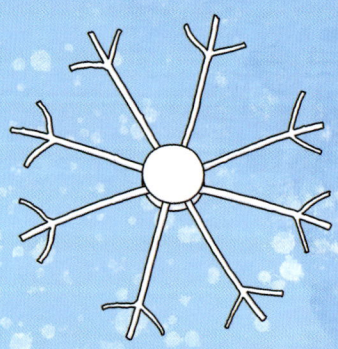

4. Glue the other circle of cardstock on top and leave to dry.

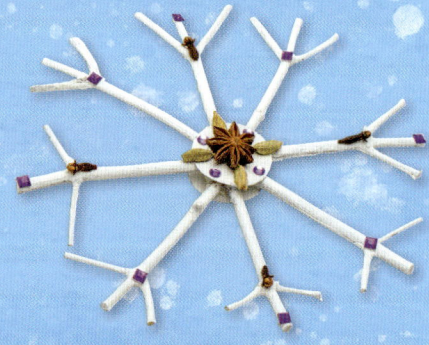

5. Glue on some dried spices. Add sparkly gems to finish your winter decoration.

Spot the Difference

Look closely at these two pictures of Ember and Flint in the winter woods. Can you spot five differences?

Answers and More

Did you spot . . . ?
- Ember's missing paw prints
- Two missing mushrooms
- The arrival of a robin
- The badger in the distance
- Two fallen pine cones

Winter is the perfect time to curl up with a book.
For more cozy reads, take a look at:

Winter Sleep: A Hibernation Story
by Sean Taylor, Alex Morss, and Cinyee Chiu

Little Homesteader: A Winter Treasury of Recipes, Crafts, and Wisdom
by Angela Ferraro-Fanning and AnneliesDraws

A World Full of Winter Stories
by Angela McAllister and Olga Baumert

Image credits pp. 26-27:
Red fox © Jim Cumming | Dreamstime.com, Fennec fox © Farinoza | Dreamstime.com,
Arctic fox © Outdoorsman | Dreamstime.com, Fox den © Geoffrey Kuchera | Dreamstime.com,
Tawny owl © Michal Pešata | Dreamstime.com, Pygmy owl © Mark Hryciw | Dreamstime.com,
Owlets © Pixtawan | Dreamstime.com, Barn owl © Isselee | Dreamstime.com.